Why Can't I Fly?

by Mrs. Baiton's, Mrs. Hannant's,
Mrs. LaBelle's, Mr. McClean's,
and Mrs. Perron's classes
with Tony Stead

capstone

Have you ever looked up at the sky and wondered what it would be like to fly? From the dawn of time, people have been in awe of insects and birds and how they fly. For hundreds of years, people tried to build wings or other machines to help them fly. In the late 1800s, the Wright brothers studied how birds fly. Finally, in 1903, the Wright brothers made the first successful airplane flight. Their flying machine was only in the air for a few seconds, but it inspired other inventors to improve the flying machine. Now we can travel across the world in a day and even blast off into space. Read on to find out more about what it takes to fly.

Airplane Parts

by Drew, Ethan, Grady, Jaxon, Kingston, Nicholas, and Owen

Airplanes are a popular way for people to travel. Airplanes have hundreds of parts that work together so people can fly and land safely. The two most important parts are the engine and the wings. Other important parts are the fuselage, landing gear, and the tail. These special parts allow us to travel through the sky.

The Engine

One of an airplane's most important parts is the engine. The engine creates thrust, which is a force that pulls an airplane forward. As the engine burns fuel, it makes exhaust, or smoke. This is the streak of white that you see behind some planes as they move across the sky.

The Fuselage

The fuselage is the biggest part of the plane. It is the main frame of the plane. It's where the passengers, the pilot, and the crew sit. It also carries suitcases and even pets!

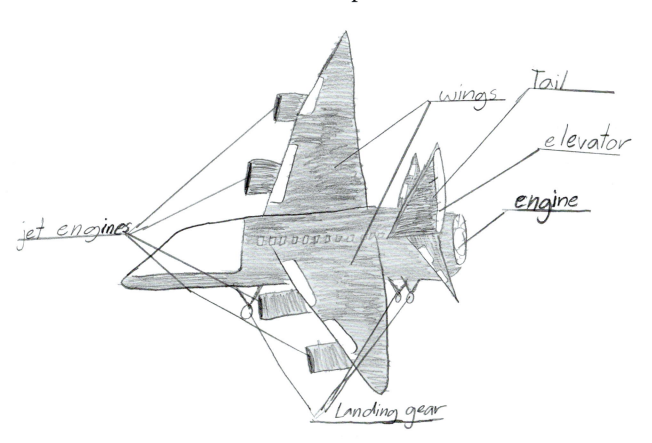

illustrated by Zander

The Landing Gear

All airplanes have landing gear. Landing gear gets tucked in on big airplanes when they are flying. Most planes have wheels for landing gear. But a plane that lands in a snowy place has skis for landing gear. Planes that land in the water have pontoons instead of wheels. Pontoons help the plane float on top of the water.

The Wings

All parts of a plane are cool, but the wings are the best! The wings are what push an airplane upward. Without the wings, an airplane wouldn't get off the ground.

The Tail and the Rudder

Did you know that every plane needs a tail? The airplane's tail is a very important part. If an airplane didn't have a tail, it wouldn't be able to fly straight. Also, it wouldn't balance very well. The rudder on a plane is connected to the tail. This part of the tail helps the airplane turn left or right. A part called the elevator helps the tail move up or down.

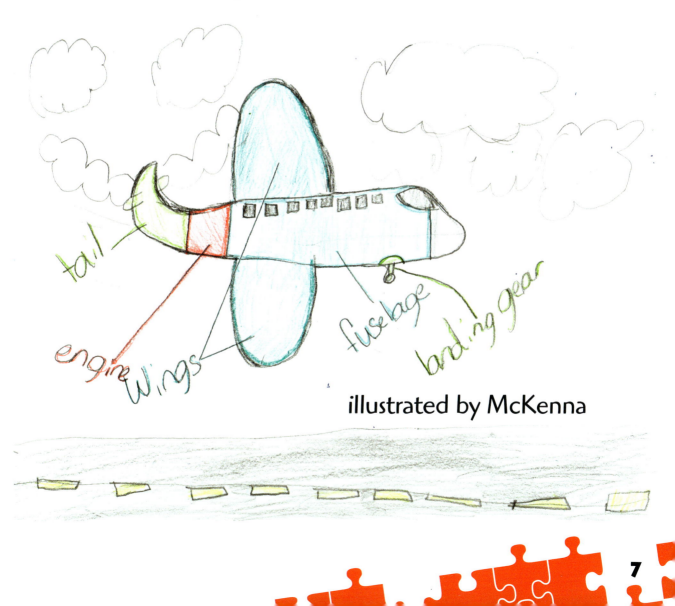

illustrated by McKenna

How Planes Fly

by Abby, Ivan, Jeremy, Jhuliana, Neal Maria, Owen, Teava, and Zander

In order for an airplane to fly, it needs lift, thrust, weight, and drag. Lift is an upward force that helps the plane get into and stay in the sky. Thrust is the force produced by the plane's engines. The thrust of the engines pushes the plane forward and creates lift.

Weight is the force of gravity pushing the plane back down toward the ground. Think about when you jump. When you jump, the force of gravity and weight will make you go back down.

Drag is the resistance of the air as the plane moves forward. Drag slows the plane down.

It's like when you ride your bike into the wind. Even if you're pedaling really fast, the force of drag from the wind will slow you down.

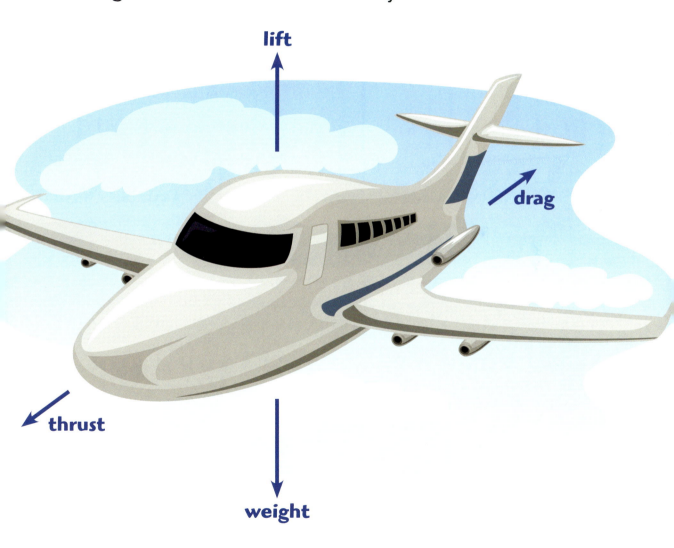

Taking Off

For a plane to take off, it needs to move fast enough so that its thrust is greater than its drag. The engine's thrust pushes the plane forward. But the drag and the weight are trying to pull it back down. To take off, the pilot increases the engine's power. When the lift is greater than the drag and weight, the plane will go forward and up, and take off.

Staying in the Air

An airplane stays in the air when lift, thrust, drag, and weight all work together. As the plane flies through the sky, air flows over and under the wings. Slower air on top of the wings makes weak pressure and less lift. Faster air pushes up on the bottom of the wings with stronger air pressure and more lift. When the air pressure and lift under the wings are stronger than the air pressure on top of the wings, the plane stays in the sky.

Landing a Plane

To go down and land, the pilot needs to decrease the engine's power. This will make the drag greater than the thrust. Then the pilot puts the landing gear or wheels down so the plane doesn't go *kerplunk* and skid across the runway. The flaps on the wings, the landing gear, and the brakes all work together to stop the plane.

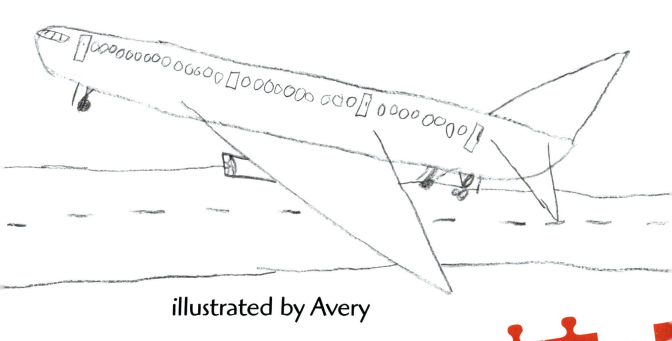

illustrated by Avery

Famous Pilots

by Claire, Hannah, Jack, Jeswin, Kaiden, Neal Maria, Tyler, and Van

The Wright Brothers

The Wright brothers are so cool! They made the first powered airplane.

The Wright brothers tried more than 150 different shapes and sizes of wings. They made hundreds of short flights between 1900 and 1902. But they needed to better control the plane, so they fixed the wings and made them stronger. They also experimented with the engine. In December 1903, when their plane first took off, it came right back down to the ground. But it rose again and stayed in the air for 59 seconds. The Wright brothers had done what nobody had ever done before!

Charles Lindbergh

Charles Lindbergh flew by himself from New York to Paris in 1927. It took him 33.5 hours! When he completed this amazing adventure to Paris, he landed in front of 150,000 people cheering him on as he became famous.

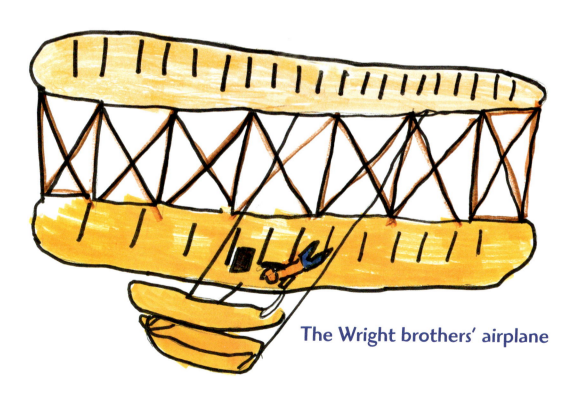

The Wright brothers' airplane

Amelia Earhart

Amelia Earhart was born in 1897 and earned her pilot's license in 1923. In 1932 she became the first woman to fly across the Atlantic Ocean by herself. It took her 14 hours and 56 minutes, but this set a record at the time.

Earhart left in 1937 to try to fly across the world. She made it two-thirds of the way, but then her plane disappeared. She was never seen or heard from again.

Bessie Coleman

Bessie Coleman was born in Texas in 1892. When Bessie was 23 years old, she became interested in flying airplanes. But flight schools in the United States wouldn't allow her to take lessons because African-Americans and women weren't allowed. Bessie was both. So she went to France to learn to fly, and in 1921 she earned her pilot's license. She was the very first African-American woman to have a pilot's license. She died in 1926 while preparing for an air show. Her bravery inspired other women and African-Americans to learn to fly.

Types of Aircraft

by Abby, Acadia, Bennett, Drew, Ethan, Grady, Jeremy, Jerzy, Leonardo, Maddison, Nicholas, Tobyn, and Tristan

Nowadays, many people have the chance to fly because inventors have created different types of aircraft to transport people.

Helicopters

Helicopters don't have wings. They have a spinning blade at the top called a propeller. They also have a tail rotor that makes them go straight. Some larger helicopters have two propellers instead of a tail rotor. Skids or wheels help helicopters land.

Helicopters can move in any direction. They can also hover, or stay in place in the air, which is really cool!

Helicopters can't fly long distances because they use up a lot of fuel quickly. But they can go just about anywhere. They can even fly to the top of a mountain to save lives when there are no roads.

Hot-Air Balloons

If you're afraid of heights, you should not hop on a hot-air balloon! A hot-air balloon is filled with gas. Hot-air balloons come in different colors, shapes, and sizes. Some are even shaped like animals or cartoon characters!

Hot-air balloons have a basket at the bottom where people can ride. I think it would be fun to ride in a hot-air balloon.

illustrated by Britney

Rockets

Rockets are awesome! Jets don't work in space, so rockets are used for space travel.

Rockets blast off from a thing called a launchpad. Rockets are used for going to places in space like the moon. Astronauts are sent to space to do things like fixing satellites. Rockets can park at a space station.

Rockets don't have wings. Rockets have things called stages, which carry some of the fuel. Fuel is also stored in fuel tanks.

After a stage is empty, it comes off to make the rocket lighter.

So what happens when the rocket needs to come back to Earth? The astronauts use the capsule. The capsule has a parachute on it. The capsule falls from space into the ocean.

Drones

A drone is a type of aircraft that can fly on its own. There are two kinds of drones. One kind is for the military and the second kind is for civilians.

Military drones were built for spying on enemies. Civilian drones are used for tracking storms, search-and-rescue missions, and watering farmers' crops. Civilian drones can even deliver packages to your door!

Blimps

Blimps are super cool aircraft that can fly. Did you know that blimps move super slowly? Blimps are similar to balloons. They float in the sky because they use gas that is lighter than air. Hydrogen gas was first used in blimps, but hydrogen explodes easily. So now helium is used instead.

Blimps are made of a frame covered in sturdy fabric. The gas sits in the gasbag and gives the blimp its shape. A blimp's crew sits in a gondola, which is underneath the blimp. To land a blimp, workers on the ground grab ropes and hold them down.

Seaplanes

Did you know that there's a type of plane that can take off and land on water? It's called a seaplane. The first seaplane was made in 1911. Seaplanes are used for firefighting, transporting people from place to place, and rescuing people at sea. Police officers also sometimes use seaplanes. Seaplanes are often used to reach islands that don't have roads.

Seaplanes need to be lightweight so they can float on top of the water. Speed lifts seaplanes up in the air.

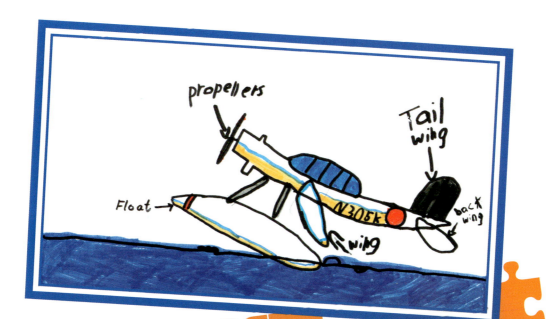

Other Things that Fly

By Abbey, Brooklyn, Brynn, Elizabeth, Skyler, and Tyler

Dragonflies

Do you know what else flies besides airplanes, helicopters, and rockets? Dragonflies. Dragonflies have two wings in the front and two in the back. Their wings sparkle in the sun and help them move quickly from place to place.

Dragonflies can hover just like a helicopter. They can fly forward and backward. They can also see forward and backward at the same time. Dragonflies are amazing!

Bees

Bees are cool, fuzzy insects that you should learn about. All bees have six legs and on the end of each leg is a tiny claw that allows them to grip. They have two feelers on their heads that they use to smell and touch.

Bees have big bodies but small wings. Before bees fly they flap their wings and shake their bodies so that they can hold their bodies up.

If bees get mad, they might sting someone. Bumblebees can sting multiple times, but honeybees can only sting once. After a honeybee stings, it dies.

So Why Can't I Fly?

First of all, we can't fly because we don't have feathers or wings. Also, our bones are too heavy, and we don't have the right body shape to fly. Aircraft can fly because they have wings, a tail, an engine, and propellers. These all help pilots take off, control their speed, steer, and land on different surfaces.

Now that aircraft have been invented, we can travel across the globe, and even leave Earth to explore the galaxy. Even though we can't use our bodies to fly, we are able to fly in an aircraft. And aircraft have certainly come a long way from when they were first invented.